For Lex, Ginger, Bonny and everlasting George.

Published in 2017 by Melbournestyle Books

Melbournestyle Books
155 Clarendon Street, South Melbourne
Victoria 3205, Australia
www.melbournestyle.com.au

All illustrations © Maree Coote 2017
Image credits last page.

National Library of Australia
Cataloguing-in-Publication entry:

    Coote, Maree, author, illustrator.

    Title: Andy Web: artist / Maree Coote.

    ISBN: 9780992491758 (hardback)

        1.Artists—Juvenile fiction.
        I. Coote, Maree, ill. II.Title

        Dewey Number: A823.4

Every effort has been made to correctly source
permissions and attribute copyright.
The publishers regret any errors or omissions.
Please send any relevant information regarding
copyright to Melbournestyle Books.

Design by Maree Coote
Printed in China

10 9 8 7 6 5 4

ANDY WEB: ARTIST

Written and illustrated by Maree Coote

Andy Web lived in the National Gallery.
He loved to draw.

At night, he came down from his web
to study the artworks.
When I grow up, I'd like to be an artist,
thought Andy.

Andy's father was an engineer,
and his mother was a spin doctor,
but Andy had always been creative.

You'll struggle with colour, worried Andy's Dad.
No spider in history has ever managed it.
Better off becoming a web developer.

Humbug, said Andy's Mum. *Art is all about*
ideas, and our Andy has a unique point of view.

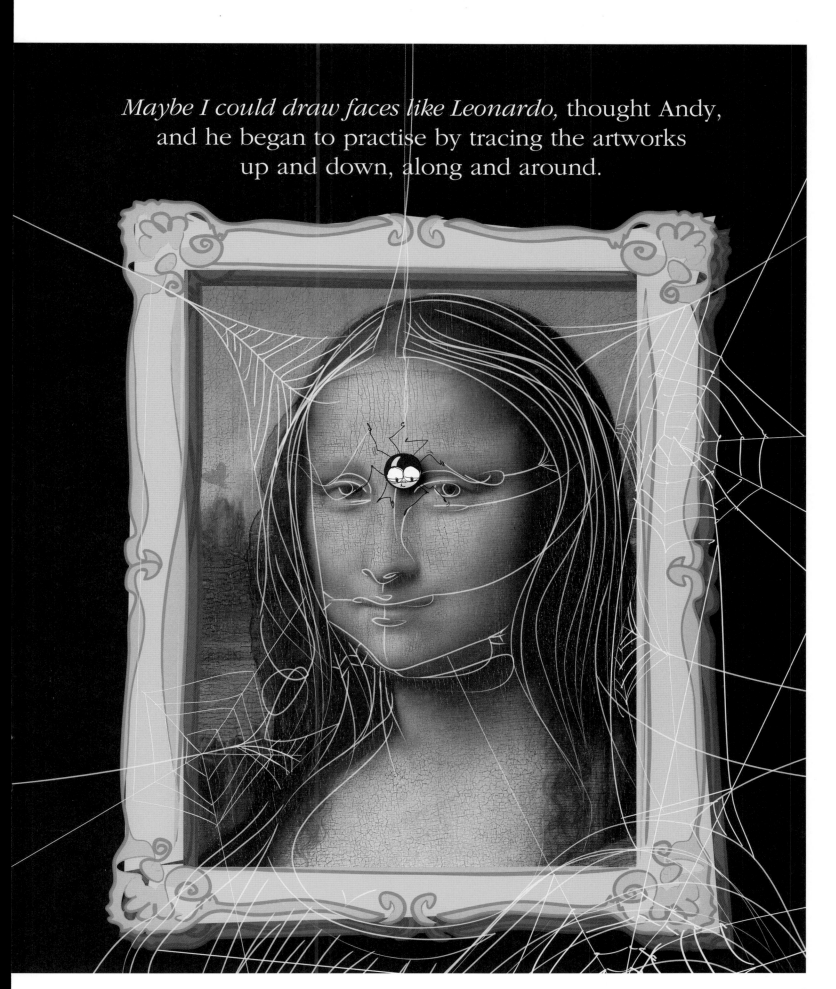

Maybe I could draw faces like Leonardo, thought Andy,
and he began to practise by tracing the artworks
up and down, along and around.

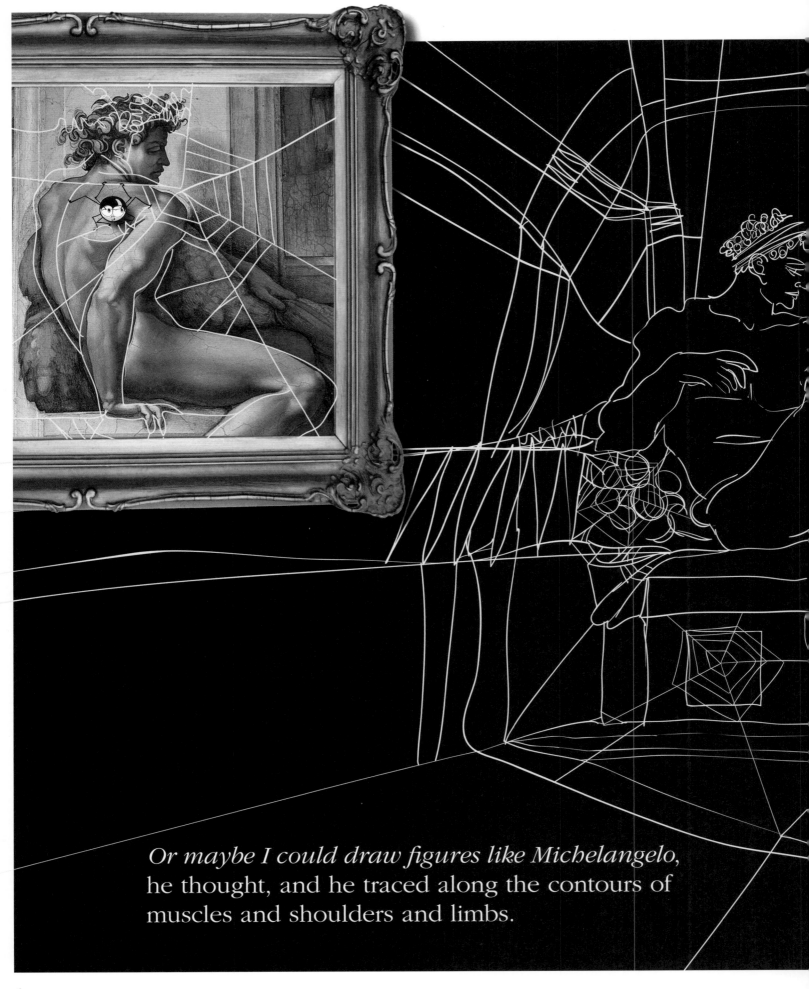

Or maybe I could draw figures like Michelangelo,
he thought, and he traced along the contours of
muscles and shoulders and limbs.

Andy took lessons from all the great painters, tracing his way across purple skies, through windows and into blue rooms...

...and surfing his web across raging seas.

The more he studied the masterpieces,
the more he learned about technique and composition.

But it was colour that
attracted Andy at every turn.

Especially red, he discovered, and he
tried his best to stay inside the lines.

Andy practised Figure Drawing with a life model,
trying hard to capture natural reality...

...and studied Abstract Art, which was nothing like reality!
His head filled with colourful ideas, but his web stayed white.

Maybe I could draw shapes from my imagination, he wondered.

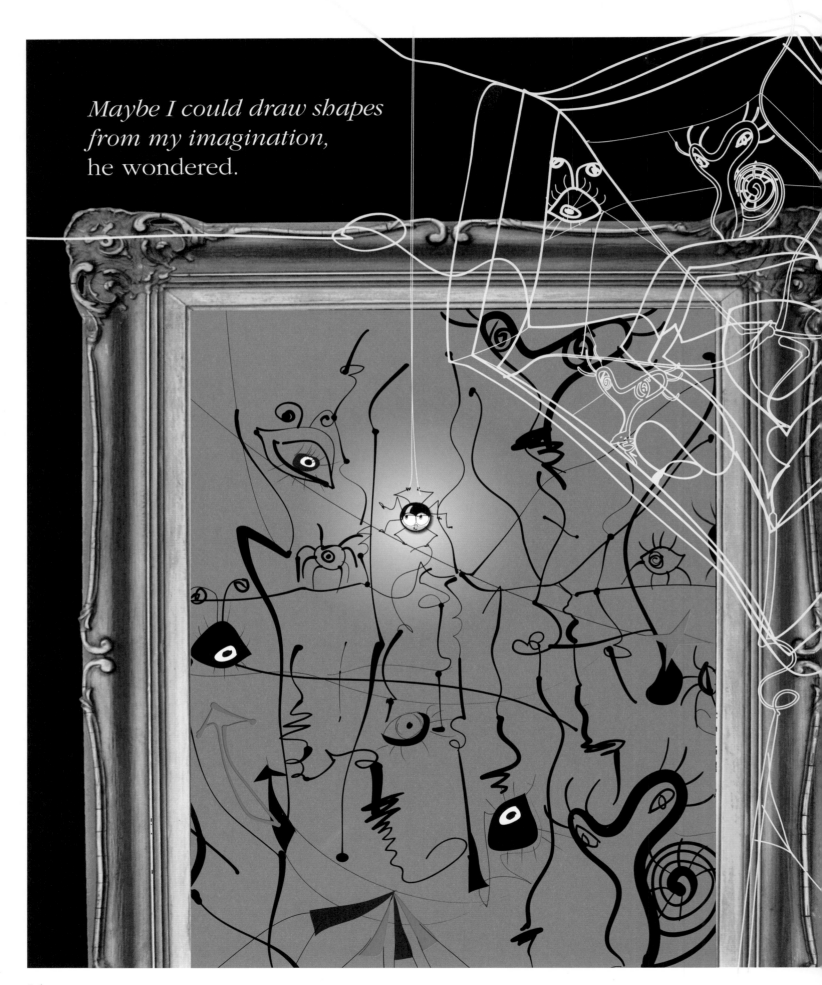

...Or do a self-portrait like Frida, he thought.
(They were both a little bit hairy, and a little bit handsome.)

And although dots were difficult,
they weren't as hard as colour,
so Andy tried his very best.

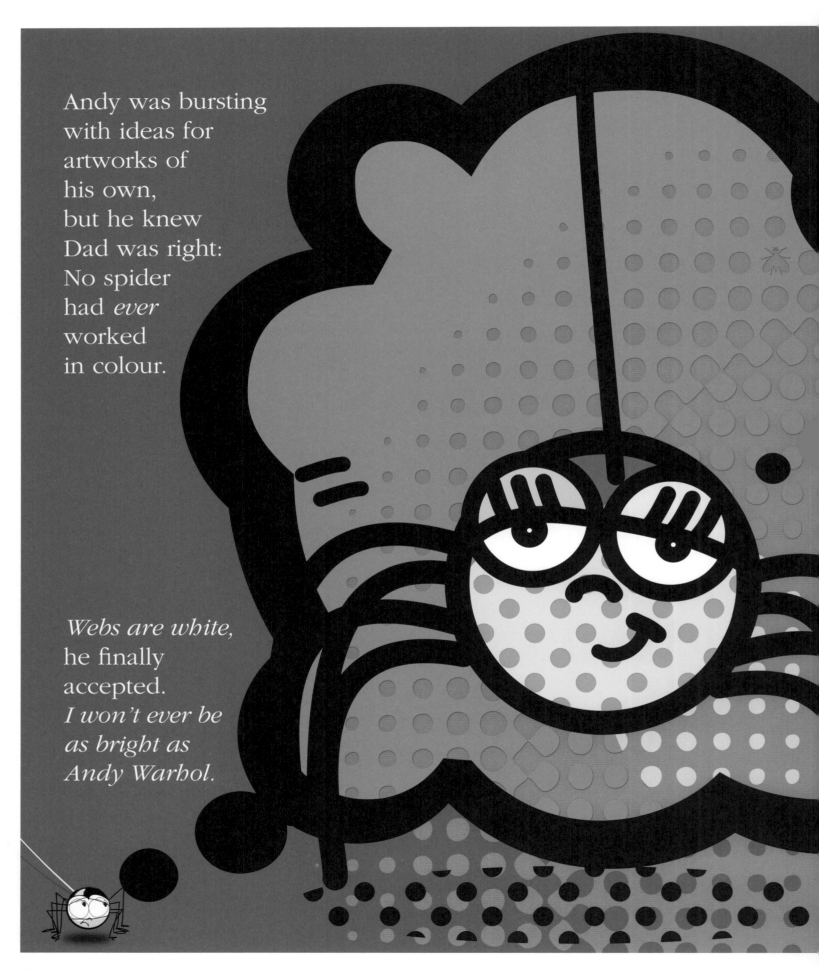

Andy was bursting with ideas for artworks of his own, but he knew Dad was right: No spider had *ever* worked in colour.

Webs are white, he finally accepted. *I won't ever be as bright as Andy Warhol.*

It was just then that Andy noticed
something wonderful in the dark gallery.

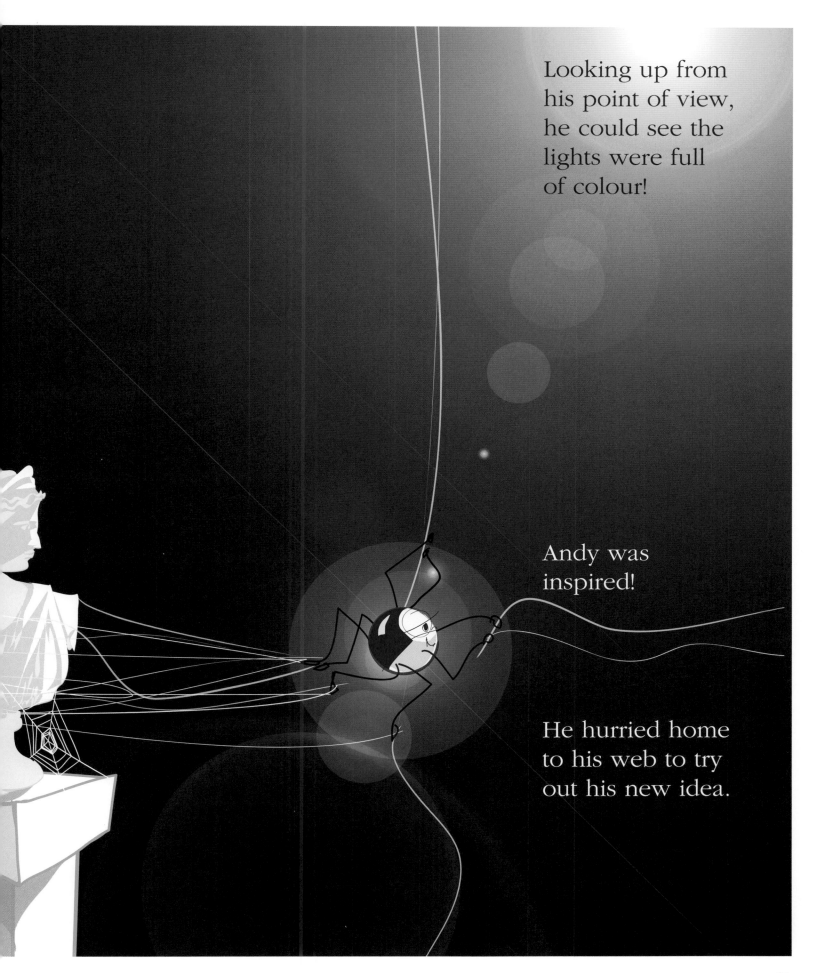

Looking up from his point of view, he could see the lights were full of colour!

Andy was inspired!

He hurried home to his web to try out his new idea.

Using the backdrop of gallery lights to fill his web with colour,
Andy mounted his own exhibition, featuring celebrity insects,
famous bugs of history, and a portrait of his mother.

22

Art is like a spider web, Andy realised. *It all depends on how you look at it*. Mum was thrilled, Dad was impressed, and everyone could see a very colourful future ahead for Andy Web: Artist.

HIDE & FIND FUN

Andy Web's favourite lunch is a nice fat fly. Can you help him find these 16 tiny flies hidden in the pages of this book?

CLEVER KIDS TEACHERS' NOTES:

Q: What is an art 'genre'?
A: A category or style of art.

Q: Can you find examples of these genres in this book:
Portraiture
Figure Drawing
Landscape
Interiors
Life Drawing
Nature Drawing
Still Life
Impressionism
Surrealism
Abstract Art
Self-Portraiture
Modern Art
Pop Art
Graphic Art

Q: Can you draw a spider in the style of Life Drawing?
Q: Can you draw a spider in the style of Abstract Art?
Q: Can you draw a spider in the style of Portraiture?

ANDY WEB'S FAVOURITE ARTISTS:

Henri Rousseau
Johannes Vermeer
Leonardo da Vinci
Michelangelo
Katsushika Hokusai
Vincent Van Gogh
Aubrey Beardsley
Edvard Munch

Howard Arkley
Piét Mondrian
Joan Miró
Pablo Picasso
Tamara de Lempicka
Frida Kahlo
Roy Lichtenstein
Andy Warhol

CLEVER KIDS TEACHERS' NOTES available online at www.cleverkids.net.au

IMAGE CREDITS:

pp.2 & p.10 EDVARD MUNCH, *The Scream*, Lithograph (detail),1895. {PD-old-auto} (PD-US) {PD-1923}
Image: Courtesy of Wellcome Images Library, London
p.3. HENRI ROUSSEAU, *The Dream*, 1910. {PD-US} {PD-1923} {PD-old-auto}
p.3 JOHANNES VERMEER, *The Girl with the Pearl Earring* (detail), c1665. {PD-old-100} {PD-Italy} {PD-US} {PD-1923} {PD-old-auto}
p.4. LEONARDO DA VINCI, *Heads of an Old Man and a Youth* (detail),1495. {PD-Italy} {PD-US} {PD-1923} {PD-old-auto}
p.4 LEONARDO DA VINCI, *Mona Lisa* (detail),1504. {PD-Italy} {PD-US} {PD-1923} {PD-old-auto}
p.7 MICHELANGELO, *Ignudo I* (detail) & *Ignudo II* (detail), Sistine Chapel 1509. {PD-Italy} {PD-US} {PD-1923} {PD-old-auto}
p.8 VINCENT VAN GOGH - Derivative works by author after *The Starry Night*, 1889 and *Bedroom at Arles*, 1888. {PD-1923}
p. 9 KATSUSHIKA HOKUSAI, *The Great Wave Off Kanagawa*, c1832. {PD-Japan} {PD-1923}
p.2 & p.10 MICHELANGELO, *Delphic Sibyl* (detail), Sistine Chapel Ceiling,1509. {PD-old-100} {PD-Italy}
p.10 MICHELANGELO, *Ignudo III* (detail), Sistine Chapel 1509. {PD-Italy} {PD-US} {PD-1923} {PD-old-auto}
p.10 STUART GILBERT, *Portrait of George Washington* (detail), 1795. {PD-US} {PD-1923} {PD-old-auto}
p.10 STUART GILBERT, *Catherine Brass Yates* (detail), 1793. {PD-US} {PD-1923} {PD-old-auto}
p.10 PAUL CEZANNE, *Rideau, Crouchon et Compotiere*,1893. {PD-US} {PD-1923} {PD-old-auto}
p.10 RAPHAELLE PEALE, *Melons and Morning Glories*,1813. {PD-US} {PD-1923} {PD-old-auto}
p.10 BALTHASAR VAN DER AST, *A Still Life of Tulips and other Flowers in a Ceramic Vase*,1625. {PD-US} {PD-1923} {PD-old-auto}

Plus original artworks by the author, after the style of and with apologies to the following artists: Aubrey Beardsley (p.2); Vincent Van Gogh (p.8); Howard Arkley (p.11); Piét Mondrian (p.11); Joan Miró (p.12); Frida Kahlo (p.13); Tamara de Lempicka (p.14); Pablo Picasso (p.15); Roy Lichtenstein (p.2 &17); Andy Warhol (p.18).

MELBOURNESTYLE BOOKS
www.melbournestyle.com.au